This book belongs to:

_____

To Karen Morris, the librarian from
Stockton Libraries who inspired this story – J.J.

In memory of my mum – S.V.

First published in Great Britain in 2015 by Andersen Press Ltd.,
20 Vauxhall Bridge Road, London SW1V 2SA.
This paperback edition first published in 2016 by Andersen Press Ltd.
Text copyright © Julia Jarman, 2015.
Illustration copyright © Susan Varley, 2015.
The rights of Julia Jarman and Susan Varley to be identified
as the author and illustrator of this work
have been asserted by them in accordance with the
Copyright, Designs and Patents Act, 1988.
All rights reserved.
Colour separated in Switzerland by Photolitho AG, Zürich.
Printed and bound in Malaysia

10   9   8   7   6   5   4   3   2   1

British Library Cataloguing in Publication Data available.
ISBN 978 1 78344 218 8

LOVELY OLD LION

JULIA JARMAN

SUSAN VARLEY

ANDERSEN PRESS

King Lion was Lenny's grandpa.
He was kind and clever but one afternoon,
when they were playing snakes and ladders,
he forgot the up and down rule.
And he couldn't remember Lenny's name.

Grandpa used to look proud and kingly,
but now he looked worried and tired.
One day he stared at Lenny's football.
He said, "What's that?" and he wouldn't
come outside for a game.

Another morning, Lenny
found his grandpa's crown
in the bin with some other
things that shouldn't have
been there.

King Lion kept getting muddled.
He even mixed up night and day.
He would say, "Goodnight, er... cub,"
and get into bed when the sun
was shining!

Grandma said, "Don't worry, Lenny. I'll play
with you. Grandpa's not himself today."
"Who is he then?" asked Lenny.
King Lion was still Grandpa!
But not so clever now, not so kingly
and sometimes not so kind.

The other animals started to notice.
Once when King Lion was singing
the same song over and over again,
Chimp laughed at him.
King Lion looked upset.
"Don't be mean!" Lenny
roared at Chimp.

Later, Hippo tried to explain
why King Lion was behaving oddly.
"He's getting old," he said, "and bits of him are
wearing out. His brain isn't working as well as
it did. That's why he keeps forgetting things."
"Then we must help him," said Lenny.
"And I know how!"

The next day, when they all met at
Lion's house, Lenny brought
his marble collection.
"It was Grandpa's," he said,
"when he was a cub."
King Lion's eyes
flickered when he
heard the marbles
rattle and he picked
up a shiny red and
white one.

"A red swirly," he said. "I beat Wildebeest with that one.
We were good mates when I was a cub."
"We still are," said Wildebeest. "Remember when we
played that trick on Croc?"

King Lion looked up.

"Did we hide his cherry bun?"

"He looked everywhere for it," laughed Wildebeest.

"And I found it," snapped Crocodile.

"With a bit of help from me," crowed Cockatoo.

The next day Wildebeest brought some photos with him.
"Remember that?" he said, pointing to one of Hippo in the bath.
"He was stuck," said King Lion, "but we pulled him out
and – SPLASH! – we all got wet." Grandpa laughed!

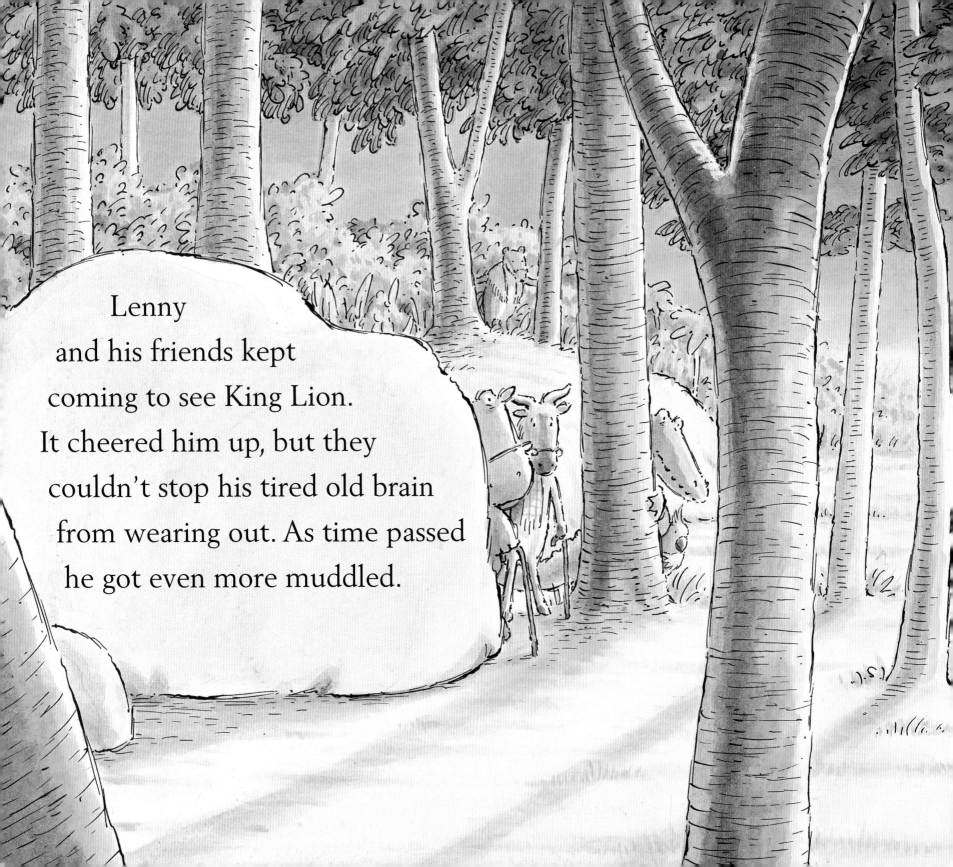

Lenny
and his friends kept
coming to see King Lion.
It cheered him up, but they
couldn't stop his tired old brain
from wearing out. As time passed
he got even more muddled.

One summer evening when Lenny found his grandpa's crown in the grass, the old lion put it on Lenny's head with his trembly paws. "You will be King one day," he said, kindly.

Now Lenny *is* king and he has a son of his own.
King Lenny is kind and clever just like his grandpa was.
He sometimes forgets things now, but he never forgets
his grandpa. He often reminds the young animals in his
kingdom to be kind to their grandpas and grandmas,
and to help them to remember.